The Sleepover Club

The Sleepover Club
Sleeps Out

by Narinder Dhami

Collins

An imprint of HarperCollinsPublishers

First published in Great Britain by Collins in 1997
Collins is an imprint of HarperCollins *Publishers* Ltd
77-85 Fulham Palace Road, Hammersmith,
London, W6 8JB

1 3 5 7 9 8 6 4 2

Text copyright © Narinder Dhami 1997

Original series characters, plotlines
and settings © Rose Impey 1997

ISBN 0 00675348 5

The author asserts the moral right to
be identified as the author of the work.

Printed and bound in Great Britain by
Caledonian International Book Manufacturing Ltd,
Glasgow G64

Sleepover Kit List

1. Sleeping bag
2. Pillow
3. Pyjamas or a nightdress
4. Slippers
5. Toothbrush, toothpaste, soap etc
6. Towel
7. Teddy
8. A creepy story
9. Food for a midnight feast: something home-made, as practice for our Brownie Cook's badge
10. Torch
11. Hairbrush
12. Hair things like a bobble or hairband, if you need them
13. Clean knickers and socks
14. Change of clothes for the next day
15. Sleepover diary

CHAPTER ONE

Hiya! It's me.

No, just for once this isn't Frankie. Bet that's given you a bit of a shock, hasn't it?

No, I'm not Fliss either. P-lease!

And I'm not Rosie. Guess again.

Wrong! It's not Lyndz.

It's me.

Kenny! Or, if you want to annoy me seriously, you can call me Laura. No-one calls me Laura except my mum when she's in a mood. If you want us to be mates, you'll never, ever let the L-word cross your lips.

I guess that by now you've realised that

you're stuck with me, instead of Frankie. Hey, you don't have to look so shocked. I don't know what Frankie's told you about me, but it's all lies. I'm not wild at all. I'm perfectly house-trained (joke). Well, most of the time, anyway.

The point is, Frankie's told you everything about the Sleepover Club up till now, and why should she have all the fun? I told her it was about time one of the rest of us got to talk to you for a change, and Frankie was cool about it. She's cool about most things. That's why she's my best mate. (I had to bribe her with a bag of Wotsits, but that's another story).

I wasn't the only one who wanted to tell you about the sleepover last Friday night. Once we'd decided that someone else instead of Frankie was going to do it, Fliss and Rosie and Lyndz were all dying to get in on the act, too. That's because our last sleepover was brilliant, one of the best ever. We had a totally radical time, and best of all, we completely trashed the M&Ms. Anyway, we argued for half-an-hour over who was going to tell you about it, and then Frankie persuaded the others that it ought to be me. That wasn't just because I gave her my Wotsits, but because it was me the M&Ms did the dirty on, and getting revenge was my idea.

Whoops, hang on a sec. I'm getting ahead of myself. I'm not as good at this as Frankie. I need a bit more practice. Hmm. D'you know what? I reckon the beginning would be a really excellent place to start.

You know all about the Sleepover Club, don't you? There's just the five of us – Frankie, Fliss, Lyndz, Rosie and me, and we sleep over at each other's houses every week-end. OK, OK, so you know all that. Don't get your intestines in a twist. I just thought that maybe if you hadn't been around before, you might not know. That's all. (You know what intestines are, don't you? They're these sort of tubes inside your stomach. I want to be a doctor, so I know about things like that. The others think I'm completely gross.)

Maybe I ought to remind you about the M&Ms as well. Remember them? Emma

Hughes and Emily Berryman? The Queen and The Goblin? The Gruesome Twosome? They're in our class at school, and they are the biggest enemies of the Sleepover Club in the whole world. If it hadn't been for the M&Ms playing that horrible trick on me, I'd never have come up with such a brilliant plan to get our own back.

Sorry, I'm doing it again. My mouth's got a mind of its own. My sister Monster-Features (my parents named her Molly, but Monster-Features sounds so-o-o much better) says if my brain was as big as my mouth, I'd be a genius, but what does she know? I never talk to her, except to fight. Yesterday I wanted to phone Frankie to talk about the sleepover, and Molly the Monster wanted to phone some stoo-pid friend of hers, and we got into a humungous argument, and I picked up the Yellow Pages and – but that's another story.

Come on, let's go, and I'll tell you what happened. And this time I'll start right at the very beginning.

CHAPTER TWO

It all started last week, on a really wet, cold and miserable day. We'd got soaked to the skin walking to school, and the only good thing was that it was a Friday. And that night we were all sleeping over at Frankie's.

"I asked my mum if we could make popcorn tonight," Frankie said as we went into the classroom.

"Really?" Fliss, who was fussing with her wet hair, looked impressed. The Sleepover Club have been banned from every kitchen in the universe since we nearly burnt her mum's house down. "What did she say?"

Frankie grinned. "She said over her dead body."

"Well, what are we going to do tonight then?" Fliss persisted. You must have sussed out by now that Fliss is just a tiny bit of a fusspot. "We could have a hair-styling contest."

"No, let's have a disco," Rosie chimed in. "I've got my new Spice Girls tape."

"Why don't we play Twister?" Lyndz suggested.

I opened my mouth to say I wanted to tell horror stories (I always want to tell horror stories at Sleepovers, but we hardly ever do, because Fliss is a bit of a wimp and gets scared), when suddenly I noticed the M&Ms coming towards us with their ears flapping.

"Hold on a minute, girls," I said, pretending to sniff the air. "There's a horrible smell around here."

The others clocked the M&Ms, and started to giggle.

"Oh, very funny," said Emma Hughes snootily. We call her the Queen because she thinks she *is* one. She goes around with her nose stuck in the air like the rest of us stink or something. If she ever went to Buckingham Palace, she'd expect the real Queen to curtsey to her. What's really irritating, though, is that all the teachers think she's wonderful.

"As if we wanted to listen to what idiots like you were saying anyway," growled Emily Berryman (The Goblin). We call her that because she's really tiny with great big eyes and a deep voice. If you put a hat on her and gave her a fishing rod, she'd look exactly like a garden gnome.

"Oh, yeah?" I said. "Well, your ears were flapping so much, you looked like you were about to take off and fly round the classroom."

"Like Dumbo," Frankie added, and we all fell about.

Emma turned red with anger. She likes to think she's perfect, but the truth is, her ears do stick out just a little bit. She opened her mouth to say something nasty in return, but just then Mrs Weaver, our teacher, came in with the register under her arm.

"Sit down, everyone," she said, looking round.

The M&Ms skipped smartly off to their table on the other side of the classroom, and I rolled my eyes at Frankie. It's s-o-o-o annoying the way the Gruesome Twosome smarm up to the teachers, and pretend to be all sweet and nice, when really they're stuck-up nerds.

Mrs Weaver sat down at her desk, and everyone stopped fidgeting and shut up. Mrs Weaver's OK, but it's best not to push her too far. Know what I mean?

"Before I do the register, I want to talk to you about our end-of-term trip next Friday." Mrs Weaver beamed round at us as if she was planning to take the whole class to EuroDisney. "We'll be going to visit the Armfield Museum, near Leicester, next Friday afternoon."

"Oh, great big fat hairy deal," I mouthed at the others. We've been to the Armfield Museum with the school a zillion times, plus our parents are always taking us there when it rains in the holidays, and there's nothing else to do. We've been there so many times, it's about as exciting as cutting your toenails. The rest of the class looked just as unimpressed as we did, and everyone started muttering and moaning under their breath.

"Awesome! The Armfield Museum!" Frankie said, just a bit sarcastically. "I'm s-o-o-o glad we're not going to Alton Towers or some other boring old theme park where we might have some fun."

"Oh, me too!" I joined in. "Who wants to go on a pathetic log flume when they could be looking at a load of broken old pots?"

Rosie was looking a bit blank.

"What's the Armfield Museum?" she asked. Rosie's fitted in so well into the Sleepover Club, that we keep forgetting she hasn't been here that long.

"Funnily enough, it's a museum," I grinned.

"It's OK, really," said Lyndz. "It's got loads of spooky stuff like Egyptian mummies."

"Yeah, but when you've seen one mummy,

you've seen them all," said Fliss gloomily, and she looked so depressed, the rest of us started to giggle.

"When you've quite finished," said Mrs Weaver, glaring round at everyone. The whole class shut up and looked at her again.

"This trip to the museum will be very different from other visits," Mrs Weaver went on. "We'll be having a guided tour, and workshop activities, but we will also be taking sleeping bags and sleeping overnight in the museum galleries."

Well, that did it. The whole class went bananas, including the Sleepover Club.

"Awesome!" Frankie said again, but this time she meant it. "A sleepover in a museum!"

"The Sleepover Club sleeps out!" Lyndz said. "Excellent!"

"D'you think they'll let us sleep in the room with the Egyptian mummies in it?" I asked eagerly. Then I clocked Fliss, who was looking a bit pea-green. "What's biting you, Flissy?"

Fliss was looking as if she was going to be sick.

"I don't think I want to sleep over in a museum," she mumbled. "It'll be scary."

"You bet it will," I said. "That's why it'll be excellent."

Fliss looked even more spooked, and Frankie stuck her elbow in my ribs.

"Ow! What I mean is, it won't be scary, Fliss. Not really. We'll all be there to look after you."

"Anyway, you can hold hands with Ryan Scott if you get scared, Fliss," Lyndz said wickedly.

Fliss turned pink. We think boys are mostly pretty r-e-e-e-volting, but Fliss has a bit of a thing about Ryan Scott, who's in our class.

"Ssshh!" Fliss whispered, glancing round at Ryan who sat at the table behind us. "He might hear you!"

"I never thought we'd be going to a sleepover with boys," I said, which started us all giggling.

"Or teachers," Rosie pointed out.

"Or the M&Ms," Lyndz said.

That stopped us laughing. We all looked across the classroom at the Gruesome

Twosome, who saw us staring, and stuck their noses in the air. I put my hands behind my ears, and waggled them at Emma, who turned purple with rage.

"We won't have to sleep in the same room as them, will we?" Rosie asked anxiously.

"I'd rather sleep with the Egyptian mummies," said Fliss. She was deadly serious too, which set us all off again.

Mrs Weaver had been trying to get us quiet again for the last five minutes, and now she'd just about managed it.

"I've got some letters for your parents with more details about the trip, which I'll give out tonight." Some people were still fidgeting with excitement and whispering to each other, and Mrs W glared at them until they stopped.

"And now it's time to settle down and get on with some work. Blue and Green groups – Maths, Yellow and Red groups – topic workbooks. Oh, and Kenny—"

I jumped. I'd been daydreaming about Armfield Museum and wondering if I'd get a chance to shut the M&Ms inside one of those big mummy cases.

"Yes, Mrs Weaver?"

"It's your turn to use the computer." Mrs Weaver had to raise her voice because everyone else was already moving round, collecting their work from their lockers. "You'd better get on with that story you started last week."

"OK, Miss." I was well pleased. I love using the computer. The only thing is, it's over the other side of the classroom, right next to the M&Ms' table.

"Hey, Emily," Emma said as I walked past them to get to the computer, "have you noticed that there's a really horrible smell around here?"

"Oh, p-*lease*!" I said, sitting down at the computer desk. "I think I've heard that one before. You two have got no imagination!"

The M&Ms both turned red.

"You think you're so clever, don't you!" Emma spluttered.

I grinned at her.

"By the way, Mrs Weaver's watching you

two," I said under my breath.

The M&Ms both jumped, looked scared and quickly opened their maths books. I nearly died laughing. Mrs Weaver was actually writing on the blackboard, and had her back to the class.

"One up to me!" I said, and I licked my finger and drew a '1' in the air. Then I turned my back on the Gruesome Twosome, and switched the computer on. I could hear them muttering to each other behind me, but I ignored them.

I found my work, and read through what I'd already written. It was a really ace story about the Loch Ness monster, and I was looking forward to finishing it and reading it at the sleepover tonight. It was so bloodthirsty, it would probably frighten Fliss into fits!

After a quarter-of-an-hour, though, I'd only written three words. Three words! At this rate I wouldn't finish the story till next Christmas. The trouble was, it was impossible to concentrate. Everyone was supposed to be working quietly, but they were so excited about the museum sleepover, that they just couldn't stop talking about it. However hard Mrs Weaver tried, she couldn't shut the class up. To make things worse, one of the maths groups was measuring all the furniture in the classroom, and they kept accidentally whacking each other with the metre sticks, like actors in a silent movie.

Like I said, it was impossible to concentrate. But I can always concentrate better when I'm using the computer if I'm eating at the same time. That was when I remembered the Opal Fruits in my jacket in the cloakroom. There were a couple of lime-green ones in there with my name on them! My mouth began to water.

I looked round. Mrs Weaver had disappeared into the book cupboard, and Ryan Scott and his sidekick Danny McCloud were fighting a duel with their metre sticks. No-one would notice if I just ducked out for a moment, and got my sweets. No, of course we aren't supposed to leave the classroom without permission, but then we're not supposed to eat sweets in class either!

"Where're you going?" Fliss asked as I sprinted over to the classroom door. That girl's got eyes in the back of her head, I swear.

"To get my Opal Fruits," I muttered, one eye fixed firmly on the book cupboard.

"Have you asked Mrs Weaver?" Fliss said sternly.

"Oh, sure," I said, "like I really want a detention that much."

"But, Kenny—" Fliss began, looking shocked. I ignored her. I was out, and back inside the classroom with my Opal Fruits hidden up my sleeve in one minute flat. Fliss looked outraged, but I winked at the others, who started laughing. Mrs Weaver had come out of the book cupboard, but she was busy examining Danny McCloud's eye where Ryan Scott had poked him with the metre stick, so she didn't notice me. I hurried back to the computer, and sat down. And that was when I got a BIG shock.

The first thing I saw was that my story had gone. Vanished. In its place was just one sentence. A single sentence repeated over and over again, from the top of the computer screen right down to the bottom.

Mrs Weaver stinks.

My jaw hit the floor. I was so shocked, I sat there staring at the computer screen, wondering what had happened. Then I realised in a flash – the M&Ms! Those nasty little nerds had done this. I just hoped I could get my story back, but first I had to get rid of the stuff on-screen before anyone saw it. I reached for the mouse, but I was already too late. I heard a voice behind me.

"How are you getting on, Kenny?"

It was Mrs Weaver. She looked at the screen, and then looked again as if she couldn't believe her eyes.

There was silence for a few moments. Somehow the rest of the class picked up that something was going on, and gradually they went quiet too, until there was a horrible silence in the whole of the room. And during that silence, the words on the screen seemed to be growing, getting bigger and bigger and blacker and blacker.

"Well, I'm surprised at you, Laura," Mrs Weaver said at last, and I could tell from her voice how annoyed she was. She didn't usually call me Laura, but this time I wasn't about to argue. "If that's how you want to waste your time, then you'd better make up for it in detention today. Now clear that rubbish off the screen, and get back to your table."

"But, Miss, I didn't write that," I began, and then I stopped. I couldn't say that the M&Ms had set me up while I went out of class (without permission) to get sweets I wasn't supposed to be eating, could I? I'd still be in trouble, whatever.

Mrs Weaver just looked at me, and walked off. I deleted all the writing, and switched the computer off. Behind me the M&Ms were giggling and nudging each other, but I ignored them, and went back to my table.

The rest of the Sleepover Club looked as shocked as I felt. Fliss was nearly crying, and Frankie, Rosie and Lyndz were as white as ghosts. As for me, I was so angry, I was boiling. I could have gone right back across the classroom, grabbed Emma Hughes and shaken her until she owned up.

"It was the M&Ms, right?" Frankie whispered in my ear as I sat down next to her. "What did they do?"

"Deleted my story, and wrote *Mrs Weaver stinks*. A zillion times." I glanced across the classroom at the M&Ms. They were smirking, and patting each other on the back. Emma saw me looking, and she licked her finger and drew a '1' in the air. I clenched my fists.

"Keep cool, Kenny," Frankie said anxiously. "Don't let her get to you."

"The rotten pigs!" said Lyndz. "We're not going to let them get away with that, are we?"

I shook my head. "No way," I muttered. "It's about time the M&Ms learned that they can't mess the Sleepover Club around."

CHAPTER THREE

"Look, we've got to decide what we're going to do," Frankie said, for about the zillionth time. "If we don't get our own back, the M&Ms'll never let us forget it."

We all nodded, but none of us said anything. We were too depressed. We were sitting in Frankie's back garden, the sun had started shining and we were eating pizza, but we were still miserable. That was because we couldn't believe the nerve of the M&Ms.

"I still can't believe they did it," Lyndz said. "I mean, the M&Ms are so goody-goody and all that."

"Yeah, I would've thought they'd be

28

scared of getting caught," Rosie agreed.

"Well, there wasn't much chance of that, was there?" Frankie pointed out. "Mrs Weaver was in the book cupboard, and everyone else was watching Ryan and Danny fighting with the metre sticks."

"And Emma was so close to the computer, she wouldn't even have had to get out of her chair," I said. "You know what I was really worried about? I thought Mrs Weaver might say I couldn't come to the museum sleepover."

"Yeah, you were lucky to get away with just a detention," agreed Frankie.

We all sat gloomily looking down at our pizzas. Not even the thought of the museum sleepover could cheer us up at the moment.

"You should have told Mrs Weaver it wasn't you, Kenny," Fliss said, also for the zillionth time.

"I did, and she didn't believe me," I said impatiently.

"You could have told her it was the

M&Ms," Fliss persisted. That girl never knows when to give up. I glared at her.

"I'm not a snitcher!"

"Anyway, Mrs Weaver wouldn't have believed you," Frankie cut in quickly. Just in time to stop me throwing a half-eaten slice of pizza at Fliss.

After what had happened, I wouldn't have got through the rest of the day if it hadn't been for the others. The M&Ms were real pigs. They kept staring at me and giggling, and looking really smug and pleased with themselves, and they made me so angry, I could have gone over there and knocked their heads together. I think Frankie and the others were a bit worried I might actually do it, because they'd stuck to my side like glue all day.

"Come on, someone must have a really good idea for getting our revenge on the M&Ms," Frankie said. "We've got to think of something."

"What have Emily and Emma done now?" Frankie's mum asked, coming towards us with a jug of lemonade. No-one had even noticed her come out of the house, and I wondered how much she'd overheard.

"Nothing!" we all said together. Well, all of us except Fliss.

"They played this really horrible trick on Kenny," she said breathlessly. "What they did was, they – OW!"

Fliss was sitting between Frankie and Lyndz, so one of them must have kicked her leg. Quite hard, too, from the look on Fliss's face. She turned pink, and shut up. I like Frankie's mum a lot, but this wasn't something we wanted to tell grown-ups about. This was private, Sleepover Club business.

Frankie's mum raised her eyebrows and waited, but we all just looked innocently at her. We're good at that. Well, Fliss goes bright red after about ten seconds, but the rest of us are brilliant at it.

I don't think Mrs Thomas was fooled, though. But she didn't say anything except, "Who wants some lemonade?" She filled our glasses, and then went back into the house.

"Who kicked me?" Fliss demanded crossly.

"Not me," Frankie said innocently.

"Nor me," said Lyndz, just as innocently.

Fliss looked from one to the other, and then gave it up as a bad job.

"I don't see why we couldn't have told Frankie's mum what happened," she grumbled, rubbing her shin.

"Because grown-ups just say things like 'Oh, ignore them'," said Frankie.

"Yeah, and they'd try to stop us getting our own back," I said. "This is our problem, and we'll decide what we're going to do about it."

"But we haven't decided anything yet," Rosie pointed out. We all sighed, and sat there in silence, sucking lemonade through our straws.

It wasn't like I hadn't thought about getting revenge on the M&Ms. In fact, I'd hardly thought about anything else all day. It would have been easy to ambush them in the girls' loos, and chuck wet paper towels at them, or do something ordinary, like putting a fake tarantula on Emma's chair. But that wouldn't be good enough. They'd set me up and got me into big trouble – and I was going to get my own back in style. That meant some serious thinking.

But at the moment, with our faces as long as a wet week-end, we weren't going to be able to decide on anything. It was time to get this sleepover going a bit. So I sucked some lemonade up through my straw, pointed it at Frankie and blew.

"Kenny!" Frankie spluttered, as lemonade squirted out all over her face. "You – you –! I'll get you for that!"

She sucked up some lemonade furiously, and blew. I ducked, and it hit Lyndz instead.

"Ow!" Lyndz squealed. "It's gone in my eye! It stings!"

To get her own back on Frankie, Lyndz began to suck some lemonade up her straw, too. But she sucked too hard, and began to choke. Rosie slapped her on the back, but a bit too much, and Lyndz pitched forward and got the straw stuck up her nose. The rest of us nearly died laughing.

I bet you can guess what happened next, can't you?

"Now – hic – I've got hiccups!" Lyndz groaned, when she was finally able to speak. "Frankie – hic – help me!"

"Try drinking from the other side of your glass," Fliss suggested. "That's supposed to work."

Lyndz picked up her glass, and turned it round.

"Like – hic – this, you mean?"

"No, dummy!" I said. "You hold the glass normally, but you try to drink from the opposite side."

Lyndz bent forward and tried to take a sip, but she tipped the glass up too much, and ended up pouring lemonade all down her T-shirt. The rest of us cried with laughter.

"This is really stupid, Fliss!" Lyndz yelled, creasing up herself. "It'll never work!"

"It already has!" said Fliss smugly.

"Come on," I said, grabbing Frankie's arm. "Let's play one of our International Gladiators' games on the lawn!"

Nobody mentioned the M&Ms and what had happened again for a long while after that. We had a few rounds of International Gladiators, then it started to rain so we went inside and played tapes and had a disco. Frankie's mum let us make popcorn after all, and we scoffed two huge bowls of it while we watched a video.

We were all tucked up in bed before we got talking about getting revenge on the M&Ms again. Frankie was in her own bed, and me and Lyndz were in the bunks, me on top and Lyndz at the bottom. Fliss was in the camp bed, and Rosie was in her sleeping bag on the floor. Mrs Thomas said goodnight and turned the light off, then we waited a few minutes and switched our torches on.

"Are we eating first?" Lyndz asked, opening her sleepover bag, and pulling out a packet of chocolate digestives. "I'm starving."

"No, wait a minute," I said. "I've been thinking!"

"You probably want to lie down and have a rest then," said Frankie.

"Ha, ha. No, I've been thinking about the M&Ms."

"I've had an idea about that," said Rosie. "Why don't we do the same to them when it's their turn to use the computer?"

"No, we've got to do something different," Frankie insisted. "We don't want to copy them."

"We could hide Emma's violin," Lyndz suggested. "Then we won't have to listen to her playing it in Assembly."

"I think we ought to get them into trouble with Mrs Weaver somehow," said Fliss. "After all, that's what they did to Kenny."

"What do you think, Kenny?" Frankie looked at me.

"I don't think we should do anything," I said.

The others looked shocked.

"What?" said Frankie. "Nothing at all?"

"No, I mean I don't think we should do anything just yet." I grinned at the others. "I think we should wait. Until the sleepover at the museum next week."

Everyone looked puzzled.

"Why?" asked Lyndz.

I shrugged. "Think about it. There's lots of spooky things in the museum, loads of places to hide and we'll be there all night. We're sure to be able to think of some way of getting our own back on the M&Ms while we're there. And best of all–!"

"What?" said the others.

"Well, we're excellent at sleepovers!" I pointed out. "We've been to loads. The M&Ms haven't."

"So we'll be one up on them before we start," said Frankie.

"We sure will!" I looked round at everyone, and we were all smiling. "The M&Ms are in for the biggest shock of their whole lives!"

CHAPTER FOUR

So we didn't do anything. We just waited. It nearly killed us, but we stuck it out. Of course, the M&Ms thought it was a big joke. They were so smug, it was unbearable. Every time we went anywhere near them, they kept making chicken noises and flapping their arms. It was really difficult not to have a go at them, I can tell you. Frankie and Fliss actually had to sit on me to stop me leaping on Emma Hughes when they were winding us up in the playground one afternoon.

But as the day of the museum sleepover got nearer, a funny thing happened. The

M&Ms started to look nervous. I don't think they'd guessed we were going to get our own back on the trip; they were just worried that we hadn't done anything to them so far, and they were beginning to wonder what we were planning. They kept on staring suspiciously at us, and I'd noticed that every time they had to open their lockers, they did it really carefully, as if they expected something nasty to fall out.

Did they really think they were gonna get away with something as ordinary as that? No chance. I had something much more special in mind for them. The trouble was, I wasn't quite sure what, yet. Not until we got to the museum.

At last the Great Day arrived.

"I'm really looking forward to this," I said to Frankie, as we waited for the coach to turn up. We were sitting on our table in the classroom. We aren't usually allowed to do that, of course, but I don't think Mrs Weaver would have noticed if we'd stood up on the tables and had a disco, because she was rushing round like she had ants in her pants, trying to organise everything.

Everyone was so excited, the noise was deafening. We all had our sleeping bags, torches, pyjamas and slippers, and big bags of food for tonight. There were some parents coming with us, as well as Mrs Weaver, so the classroom was packed.

"Oh, this is going to be ace," said Rosie happily. "I can't wait to see the Egyptian mummies!"

Fliss looked a bit sick again.

"As long as we don't have to sleep in the same room as them," she said firmly.

"We'll see about that," I said under my breath to Frankie, who grinned and winked at me.

"I wonder who'll be our group leader?" Lyndz said. "I hope we don't get Mrs Weaver. She's got eyes in the back of her head."

"Yeah, we don't want anyone too smart, do we?" I lowered my voice. "Not if we're going after the M&Ms."

"Maybe we'll get one of the parents," said

Fliss.

"Yeah, isn't Alana Banana's mum coming?" said Frankie. "Alana's pretty dozy, so maybe her mum is, too."

We all looked over at Alana Banana. Banana isn't really her surname. It's Palmer. Alana Banana's pretty harmless, but she does hang around with the M&Ms sometimes, which makes her sort of our enemy. Except that she's too clueless to bother us much.

"Mrs Banana isn't here yet, is she?" said Lyndz, looking round.

"No, and anyway, she'll probably be looking after Alana's group," Frankie pointed out.

Just then we realised that Mrs Weaver was trying to get everybody's attention by yelling "QUIET!" and waving her clipboard around like a flag. We all shut up and looked at her.

"Right, the coach will be here in about ten minutes," Mrs Weaver said briskly. "Before we go, I'll tell you the name of the adult who's in charge of your group." She looked over at the M&Ms. "Emma Hughes' group, you'll be with me."

Frankie glanced at me, and pulled a face. At least we weren't in Mrs Weaver's group – that would have been a mega disaster – but the M&Ms were. That might make our plans for revenge a little bit tricky. It depended who our group leader was.

"Francesca Thomas's group." Mrs Weaver looked over at us. "You'll be with Miss Hill."

We all cheered. If I tell you that Miss Hill's a student teacher, you'll know why. You can get away with murder with a student teacher. Miss Hill, who was standing next to Mrs Weaver, turned bright pink. She probably thought we were cheering because we liked her so much. We did like her. But we liked her even more because she wasn't as clued up as Mrs W.

"Excellent!" I whispered in Frankie's ear. "Now we're all set!"

"Alana Palmer's group," Mrs Weaver went on. "You'll be with Alana's mum – where is your mum, by the way, Alana?"

Alana Banana frowned.

"She can't come, Miss."

Mrs Weaver nearly dropped down dead with shock.

"What do you mean, she can't come? It was all arranged!"

"I told you this morning that she couldn't come," said Alana.

Mrs Weaver turned purple. "No, you did not tell me, Alana!"

Alana Banana looked puzzled. "Oh, didn't I? I thought I did!"

I've never heard a teacher say a rude word, but I think Mrs Weaver came pretty close.

"I'll have to go and see who I can round up," she said to Miss Hill. "We've got to have one adult for each group of five children. Just keep an eye on them, will you?"

Mrs Weaver raced out of the room faster than Linford Christie, and headed off down the corridor.

"Now don't make too much noise," said Miss Hill, but nobody could hear her because we were all chattering.

"That Alana Banana's a real nerd," said

Frankie. "It'd serve her right if Mrs Weaver left her group behind."

Mrs Weaver didn't come back for ages. We were all beginning to get a bit fed up, when we saw the coach pull into the playground.

"Here's the coach!" yelled Rosie. "Time to go!"

Everyone cheered, grabbed their bags and headed for the door.

"I think we ought to wait for Mrs Weaver," said Miss Hill timidly, but no-one listened to her. It was a good job she wasn't standing in front of the door either, or she'd probably have been trampled on. The whole class piled out of the classroom, and charged for the coach. The driver saw us coming, looked a bit nervous and shut the doors, so we had to queue up instead. Luckily the Sleepover Club managed to get to the front.

"I want to sit at the back," I said.

Fliss groaned. "I get sick on the back seat. Anyway, there's only room for four."

"Oh, we can all sit together if we squash up," said Lyndz.

"My group wants to sit at the back," said Ryan Scott, who was standing behind us, trying to push in.

Fliss giggled, but the rest of us glared at him.

"No chance," I said. Then, right at that moment, I noticed Frankie's mum coming across the playground towards us.

"Hey, Frankie," I said, elbowing her in the ribs. "What have you forgotten?"

"What?" Frankie looked puzzled.

"You must have forgotten something," I teased her. "Here's your mum."

Frankie frowned. "What's she doing here?"

"Will you please queue up properly without pushing, or I'll send you back into class!" yelled Mrs Weaver, who'd just come out into the playground. "Sort yourselves out, please. Oh, Mrs Thomas, there you are. Thank you for filling in at such short notice."

We almost dropped down dead with shock. Frankie's mum was coming with us? That was seriously bad news. Mrs Thomas is a just bit too sharp to have around when you're planning something naughty.

"Hello, girls," said Frankie's mum. "You don't have to look quite so pleased to see me."

"Don't panic," I whispered to the others, as Mrs Weaver began telling Mrs Thomas the arrangements for the trip. "At least we're not in her group."

"Oh, Frankie," said Mrs Weaver, "I thought you'd want to be in your mum's group, so I've asked Miss Hill to take over Alana's group instead. Right, I think we're just about ready to get on the coach now."

We were all so stunned, we let Ryan Scott and his group push past us to grab the back seat. The M&Ms with Mrs Weaver, and us with Frankie's mum – were we ever going to get a chance to put our plan of revenge into action?

"Come on, girls, let's get on the coach," said Mrs Thomas. "This is going to be fun. Isn't it?"

CHAPTER FIVE

So there we were, stuck with Frankie's mum, and there wasn't anything we could do about it. We couldn't even talk amongst ourselves, because Mrs Thomas got on the coach right behind us. Luckily, she sat right at the front next to Mrs Weaver, while we scuttled off down towards the back.

"Better luck next time, girls," said Ryan Scott smugly from the back row. We ignored him, and slid into some empty seats, me next to Fliss, and Lyndz, Rosie and Frankie squashed in together.

"I can't believe my mum's coming with

us," Frankie groaned. "Why did she have to have a day off work today?"

"What are we going to do now then?" asked Fliss urgently.

"Maybe we ought to forget the whole thing," Rosie muttered.

"Rosie's right," Lyndz agreed. "This is getting more and more dodgy."

"No way!" I said. "Don't be a bunch of wimps."

The others looked at me. They weren't convinced.

"It's too risky," Frankie said at last. "The museum's going to be crawling with grown-ups. And one of them will be my mum."

"So?" I shrugged. "There are always grown-ups around when we have our sleepovers. Have we ever let that stop us doing exactly what we want?"

"Kenny's right," said Fliss. "We can't give up now."

If I hadn't already been sitting down, I think I would have fallen down with shock. Fliss was the last person I would've expected to back me up.

"Thanks, Fliss!" I said, giving her a friendly punch on the arm.

"Ow!" Fliss clutched her elbow. "Do you mind!"

"D'you think we can get away with it?" Lyndz asked doubtfully.

"Yeah, I think we should go for it!" I said. "Leave it to me. I'll think of something that'll completely trash the M&Ms, and fool all the grown-ups."

The others grinned.

"OK, then, Kenny," said Frankie. "But it'd better not be anything too wild, because if my mum finds out we're up to something, I'm dead."

From the moment the coach pulled up outside Armfield Museum, and we all piled out, I was on the look out for possibilities. The museum's a big place – it's in a kind of old country house with lots of rooms – and I was pretty sure that, sooner or later, I'd get a brilliant idea. I didn't know what yet, but I'd know when I did. If you see what I mean.

We all followed Mrs Weaver into the museum, where we left our bags in the cloakroom.

"Get into your groups now, please," called Mrs Weaver. "The museum's Education Officer is going to give us a guided tour."

There was a lot of pushing and shoving and giggling as everyone tried to get back into their groups. All the parents were fussing, and trying to get the kids who were with them to stand in rows and shut up. Frankie's mum didn't fuss, though. She just looked us over, said, "Everyone all right?", and then left us alone.

"Your mum's so cool, Frankie," Lyndz whispered. "For a mum, I mean."

"Yeah, but she won't be so cool if she figures out we're planning a raid on the M&Ms," Frankie whispered back. "She'll be steaming mad."

"We'll have to make sure she doesn't find out then, won't we?" I said with a wink.

The museum Education Officer, Mrs Saunders, took us on the guided tour. She made it pretty interesting by telling us loads of stories and jokes about the different things the museum had, but I wasn't really listening. That was because 1) I'd been on the guided tour about a zillion times before, and 2) I was busy keeping my eyes open for something I could use to blow the M&Ms away.

At first I didn't see anything. We went into the Costume Rooms, the Doll Gallery, the Roman Room and all the other rooms, and I was starting to get worried. Maybe I'd made a mistake thinking that the museum would be a good place to play a trick on the M&Ms!

It wasn't until we went into the last room, which was the Egyptian Room, that things really started to hot up. There were loads of glass cases round the wall with things in them like old pots, gold jewellery and big stone cats. And right in the middle, lying on a platform, were six big, painted mummy cases. One of them had glass in the top, and if you looked through it, you could see the bandaged mummy lying inside. Mrs Saunders started telling us about how the Egyptians used to make dead bodies into mummies by taking out all their insides, and using a special liquid, so the bodies didn't rot away. Fliss didn't like that one bit. She turned green, and went to hide behind Frankie's mum. I knew all about mummies, but I didn't mind hearing it again, because it was so gruesome. So it took me a little while to suss out that Fliss wasn't the only one who was looking a bit icky. I nudged Frankie.

"Look at the M&Ms," I whispered in her ear.

Emma and Emily were both looking a bit sick. Not only that, they both looked scared, and they were standing really close to Mrs Weaver. They were both staring at the mummy cases as if they expected a mummy to jump out there and then, and grab them, like something in a horror film.

"They look like they're wetting themselves," Frankie whispered back.

"They are," I said. "And I think I've just sussed out our plan of revenge."

"What?" asked Rosie eagerly.

I opened my mouth to tell them, saw Frankie's mum looking at us and decided to wait till later. We were taken off to the museum café to have some juice and biscuits, and Frankie's mum left us on our own, while she went to talk to Mrs Saunders. That gave us a chance to get stuck into our plans.

"I've had this radical idea," I said, after I'd looked over my shoulder to check that the M&Ms (and Mrs Weaver) were nowhere around. "Did you see how freaked out the Gruesome Twosome were by the mummies?"

Fliss shook her head. "I didn't notice."

"That's because you were hiding behind Frankie's mum," said Lyndz.

"Well, anyway, they were dead scared," I went on. "And I reckon that's how we can get our own back on them."

"How?" said the others together.

I hadn't really sussed out the details yet, but I'd had one idea which I thought was excellent.

53

"Well," I said, "I thought I could hide inside one of the mummy cases and – "

I didn't get a chance to say any more, because the others nearly had a fit.

"Get serious, Kenny!" said Frankie. "Those mummy cases are worth loads of money! If you damage one of them – "

"We'll be paying for it out of our pocket money for the next zillion years," Lyndz finished off.

Fliss was almost fainting with fear.

"And what if you got stuck inside?" she gasped.

"Yeah, you'd probably suffocate," Rosie pointed out anxiously.

"Oh, all right!" I said crossly. I guess I hadn't really thought this thing through. "OK, stupid idea. But I still think we can use the mummies to get back at the M&Ms..."

And I was right. After we'd finished our juice and biscuits, Mrs Saunders took us to the activities room. There were paints, paper, glue and scissors on the tables, as well as loads of big cardboard boxes.

"We're going to make some masks," announced Mrs Saunders. "You can choose to make a mask of anything you've seen in the museum today, and I've got some postcards here to help you. If anyone would like to copy one of the painted faces of the Egyptian mummies, that would make rather a good mask."

And then, like a light bulb being switched on above my head, THAT was when I got my brilliant idea.

CHAPTER SIX

I couldn't tell the others about my totally brilliant plan straightaway, because everyone was rushing round the room, grabbing cardboard boxes and glue and scissors. There was also a fight over the postcards, because almost everyone wanted to make a mummy mask, so Mrs Saunders had to go off to the museum shop to fetch some more. That all fitted in nicely with my plan.

"OK, Kenny," Frankie said, when we were all sitting round our worktable, heaped with model-making materials. "You've been grinning all over your face for the last five minutes. What's going on?"

"I've got it!" I said, lowering my voice, just in case. There was more noise going on in the room than in the monkey house at the zoo, but it was best to be on the safe side. "I've thought of something that's going to send the M&Ms off their heads!"

"What?" the others asked eagerly.

I shrugged. I was enjoying keeping them in suspense.

"Tell you later," I said. "I'm going to make my mask first."

The others looked disappointed.

"Oh, go on, Kenny, tell us!" begged Fliss.

"I bet she hasn't really thought of a plan, anyway," said Frankie.

I grinned, and stuck my tongue out at her.

"Oh, yes, I have, Francesca Thomas. But, like I said, I'll tell you later." I turned to Lyndz. I was going to need help to get my plan going, and I reckoned Lyndz would be best. "Let's work together, Lyndz."

"All right," Lyndz agreed cheerfully. "Which mask do you want to make then?"

"This one." I showed her the postcard I'd chosen. It was one of the painted mummy faces, the one which I thought was the scariest. It had a gold and blue headdress, and big, staring eyes, which were outlined in black.

"Oh, that's gross!" Fliss shuddered. "I wouldn't make one of those for a zillion pounds. I'm going to make a mask of one of the Victorian dolls in the doll gallery."

"Me and Frankie'll help you," Rosie offered.

Frankie pulled a face. "I'd rather make a mummy mask, like Kenny and Lyndz."

"OK, you can help us, then." I picked up a cardboard box, and put it over my head. It was so big, it covered my top half down to my shoulders. "I reckon this'll do, for starters."

"It suits you," Frankie said. "But maybe we ought to get on with the mask."

"Ha, ha," I said from inside the box. "I mean, we can make the mask out of this."

I lifted the box off, just as the M&Ms were walking past our table.

"Ooh, Emily!" Emma Hughes squealed,

rolling her eyes dramatically. "Look at that horrible mask Kenny's wearing!"

"No, I think that's just her face, isn't it?" said Emily with a stupid grin, right on cue, and they both started laughing like drains.

"You two are so funny," I said. "If you want a really good laugh, why don't you take a look at yourselves in a mirror?"

That wiped the grins off their faces, and the others began to giggle.

"Hey, Emma," The Queen was determined to have the last word, "what's Kenny's favourite food?"

"Oh, that's got to be Kentucky Fried Chicken," burbled The Goblin, and the two of them walked off, flapping their arms and squawking.

"I hope this plan of yours is totally brilliant, Kenny," said Frankie, clenching her fists, "Because the Gruesome Twosome are getting well out of control."

"Oh, it is," I said confidently. "Come on, let's get on with our mask."

Even with Frankie helping me and Lyndz, it

was a bit of a rush to get the mask finished. But by the time Mrs Thomas told us to start tidying up because it was time to eat, the mask was just about ready. I'd wanted Lyndz to help me because she's totally *coo*-ell at arty stuff, and she'd done all the cutting and sticking of the cardboard box, to make it into the shape of the mummy's headdress. Frankie's not bad at art either, and she'd painted the mummy's face on. It looked just like the real thing. I'm pathetic at anything like that, so I'd stuck to the easy bits, painting the blue and gold stripes on the headdress.

"Hey, that's excellent," said Rosie, when she and Fliss came over to take a look. "Can I try it on?"

I shook my head. "No, the paint's still a bit wet."

Fliss shuddered. "It looks just like the real one," she said.

"I know," I said. "If you saw it in the dark, in the middle of the night, you'd be dead scared, wouldn't you?"

Fliss nodded. "I think I'd die!"

I grinned. "I reckon that mask would scare anybody!" I looked round at the others to see if they'd picked up what I meant. But they were all staring at me blankly.

Then Frankie grinned. "You're going to use the mask to frighten the M&Ms out of their skins!" she said.

"Right first time," I agreed. I looked round at the others. "Is that a totally ace plan or what?"

"That's brilliant!" said Rosie and Lyndz together. Only Fliss looked a bit nervous.

"Kenny, I don't think that's a very good idea –" she began, but she didn't get a chance to say any more, because Mrs Weaver called for silence.

"Leave your masks on the tables to dry, and you can take them home with you tomorrow morning," she said. "Now we have to decide which groups are sleeping where tonight." Everyone started muttering and whispering in excited voices. As far as I could make out, almost every kid in the class wanted to sleep over in the Egyptian room with the mummies.

Mrs Weaver picked up her clipboard, and studied it.

"Would any group like to sleep in the Doll Gallery?" she asked hopefully.

The M&Ms's hands went up. So did Fliss's. Well, it did until Frankie grabbed her wrist, and pulled it down.

"Emma, I think your hand was up first," said Mrs Weaver. "Your group can go and get your bags, and take them to the gallery now."

Fliss glared at Frankie. "I wanted to sleep in the Doll Gallery," she moaned.

We all ignored her.

"Who'd like to sleep in the Egyptian room?" Mrs Weaver went on.

My hand flew up into the air, and so did about twenty-five others.

"Kenny, I think you were first," said Mrs Weaver. Everyone else in the class groaned loudly. "Your group can go and collect your bags."

"Go and get your things, girls," said Mrs Thomas, coming up behind us. "I'm going to the café to have a cup of tea."

We went to the cloakroom to get our stuff, and then we carried it down the corridor to the Egyptian room. We dumped them in a corner, and I pulled the door shut, so that we were finally on our own, away from all the interfering grown-ups.

"Right!" I said. "Now we can talk about Operation Gruesome Twosome!"

Fliss was looking nervously around the room.

"I'm never going to get to sleep in here!" she muttered.

"Don't worry, Fliss," said Frankie, "the mummies don't make any noise."

"No," I agreed, "except when they're moaning and wailing and trying to frighten people to death."

Fliss groaned. "Stop it, Kenny!"

"So, what's the plan, Kenny?" asked Lyndz.

I already had it all worked out.

"We wait till Frankie's mum's asleep, then

63

we sneak out, get the mask and take it to the doll gallery." I grinned round at the others. "Then we tap it against the window, and frighten the M&Ms out of their stupid little skins!"

Everyone started giggling.

"What about Mrs Weaver?" asked Lyndz. "She's going to be in with the M&Ms, isn't she?"

I shrugged. "I'll have the mask on, so even if she wakes up, she won't know it's me. The rest of you will have to make sure you keep out of sight."

"Won't Mrs Weaver recognise your mask?" asked Rosie.

I shook my head. "No, about half the class have made the same mask we did. Anyway, it's going to be pretty dark."

"What about Frankie's mum?" asked Fliss. "She might wake up when we sneak out."

"We'll have to risk it," I said. "The other thing is, we'll have to wait until we're sure everyone's asleep, not just Frankie's mum."

"I'll never be able to keep awake," said Fliss.

"I could set my watch alarm," offered Rosie.

"Yeah, and have Frankie's mum wake up as well?" I pointed out.

"Oh, I can wake everyone up," Lyndz said confidently. "I've got this brilliant system for getting myself up without an alarm clock. You just bang your head on your pillow six times if you want to wake up at six o'clock, and it works. It's magic!"

"Right, let's make it two o'clock then," I said. "Now we're set!"

But this is the Sleepover Club, right? And nothing's ever that simple!

CHAPTER SEVEN

I opened my eyes, and blinked. For a minute, I couldn't remember where I was. Then, through the darkness I saw the shadows of the mummy cases all lined up on the platform. I wasn't scared, though. I mean, I have to look at Molly-the-Monster's ugly face every morning. So why should I be scared of a load of old mummies?

I didn't know how long I'd been asleep, but Lyndz hadn't woken us up yet, so it couldn't have been very long. I looked round at the others. They were all asleep, curled up in their sleeping bags. We were all lying in a row

66

next to the platform which had the mummy cases on. Guess who was the furthest away? Yeah, go to the top of the class. Flissy Baby wasn't taking any chances, just in case one of the mummies fancied a midnight feast.

I raised myself on my elbow, and looked cautiously across the room. Frankie's mum was over the other side of the platform, and it looked like she was fast asleep, too. She'd been a bit surprised last night that we were so keen to go to bed, and that we didn't want to stay awake for ages chatting, like everyone else was doing. Still, I don't think she suspected anything was going on!

The museum was dead quiet now, though. Everyone had to be asleep, even Ryan Scott's group, who were in the Roman Room next door. They'd kept trying to frighten us after lights out by tapping on the wall. Boys. They're s-o-o-o-o pathetic.

I rolled over, and picked up my watch, and my eyes nearly popped right out of my head. Half past four!!! What had happened to Lyndz's 'brilliant' system to wake everybody up? I leaned over and shook Frankie, who was lying next to me. When she opened her eyes, I waved my watch in front of her face.

"It's half-past four!" I mouthed silently, pointing at the door.

Frankie nodded, and shook Rosie, who was next to her. Rosie woke Lyndz up, and Lyndz sat up, yawning and looking puzzled.

"It's not two o'clock, is it?" she whispered.

"No, it's half-past four!" I whispered back. "Great waking-up system, Lyndz!"

"We'd better go," Frankie said, sliding out of her sleeping bag. "It'll be getting light soon."

Lyndz rolled over, and poked Fliss. Fliss opened her eyes, took one look at the mummy cases, and let out a little scream. Lyndz lunged across and tried to stop her, but it was too late.

We all froze, waiting for Frankie's mum to sit up and ask us what was going on. But she didn't. We heard her roll over in her sleeping bag, and then there was silence.

We didn't even dare sigh with relief. Instead we just got to our feet, and tiptoed over to the door, which was so heavy, Frankie and I had to hold it open to let everyone slip silently out. When we were all safely outside in the corridor, we sighed with relief.

"Sorry," Fliss said shakily. "The mummies nearly scared me to death."

"From now on, we've got to be really quiet," I whispered. "If anyone wakes up, we're dead."

We had to get the mask first, so we tiptoed down the dimly-lit corridor to the activities room, hardly daring to breathe. We had to go past the Roman Room, where Ryan Scott's group were sleeping, and past the Art Gallery, where Alana Banana's group were with Miss Hill. Luckily, the doors were closed.

The activities room was really dark, but we didn't dare put the light on. The others waited by the door, while I groped my way round the tables, trying to find our mask. Frankie was holding the door open, so there was a bit of light from the corridor, but not much.

"Hurry up, Kenny," Fliss was moaning, "if we get caught, Mrs Weaver'll never let us go on another school trip ever again."

"Oh, great big fat hairy deal," I muttered. I was feeling my way round the tables, and knocking things over, including a pot of glue. "Oh, rats! Now I've got glue all over my hand!"

"Never mind that," said Frankie. "Just get a move on!"

I found the mask, and hurried back over to the door. "Got it!" I said triumphantly.

Fliss took one look at the mask, and stepped behind Frankie.

"Keep that thing away from me, Kenny!" she hissed, giving me a dirty look.

"It's that scary, huh?" I slipped the mask over my head. "Let's see what it looks like when it's on."

Lyndz had neatly cut out the big eyes, so that I could see through them. The others looked impressed (except Fliss, of course).

"It's brilliant!" said Frankie. "The M&Ms are going to wet themselves!"

"Serves them right!" said Rosie.

I took the mask off again, and put it under my arm.

"Come on, then. What's the quickest way to

the Doll Gallery?"

"We can take a short cut through the Costume Rooms," said Fliss.

So we tiptoed along the corridor to the Costume Rooms. We got lost a few times, because there were so many twists and turns, but eventually we made it. Frankie pushed the door open a little way, and then froze.

"What's biting you?" I began.

"SSHHH!" Frankie hissed. "There's someone in there!"

"It's a ghost!" moaned Fliss, clutching Lyndz's arm.

"Ow!" said Lyndz. "Let go, you're hurting me!"

"QUIET!" ordered Frankie, in a whisper that was louder than anyone. She let the door swing softly back into place. "Caroline Powell's group's in there, with her mum. We'll have to go a different way."

I thought for a minute. It was lucky we'd been to the museum so many times before, and knew our way around.

"We'll have to double back, and cut through

71

that room that's got all the statues in it. Come on."

We hurried back down the corridor, and after a few false starts, we made it to the right room. Frankie pulled the door open just a bit, and checked that none of our class were sleeping inside, then we all went in. It was a big room, with a large window in the ceiling, and a light had been left on, although it wasn't very bright. There were white stone statues of people and animals all round the room. Some were just heads, but others were really big, reaching almost to the ceiling.

"I don't like this," said Fliss nervously, as we walked through the room towards the door on the opposite side. "They're all staring at me."

"They're statues, dummy," I said. "They're not real."

"They might be," said Fliss. "They might come to life at night."

"Oh, grow up, Flissy," I said impatiently. "Anway, even if they did, what do you think they're going to do?"

"They'd probably go and find some clothes," said Rosie, with a grin. "They look pretty cold."

That made Fliss giggle. "They could definitely do with some underwear," she said, and the others started to giggle too.

"Oh, grow up and shut up!" I sighed, reaching for the door. "Everyone ready?"

Fliss was still giggling, so I gave her the evil eye until she stopped. Then we slipped out into the corridor.

"Which way do we go now?" Rosie asked.

"That way," said Frankie, pointing right.

"That way," said Fliss at exactly the same moment, pointing left.

We went right, because Frankie usually knows best. But we had to go quite a long way down the corridor before we got to the Doll Gallery.

"This is it!" I said quietly, as we stopped in front of the doors. My heart was pounding with excitement. I'd waited a long time to get my revenge on the M&Ms, and now I was going to enjoy it. "I'm going to take a look inside, and find out where the M&Ms are."

"Be careful," said Frankie.

I laid the mask carefully on the floor, and put my face to the glass at the top of the door. I could just about see in. The room was quite dark, but someone had left their torch on, so I got a pretty good view. The dolls were in glass cases all around the walls, and there were six sleeping bags dotted in different places around the room. The M&Ms were in the perfect place, not far from the door where I was looking in. Best of all, Mrs Weaver was right over the other side of the room.

"Ace!" I whispered to the others. "The M&Ms are right here, and Mrs Weaver's miles away!"

"I want to see!" said Fliss.

"Me too," said Rosie. "I want to watch the M&Ms faces when they see Kenny in the mask!"

I shook my head. "No way," I said. "They'll see you for sure."

"Hang on a minute," said Frankie. "We could

go round the side, and look through the curtains."

There was a long row of windows at the side of the gallery, where the curtains had been drawn, but they didn't quite meet.

"Go on, then," I hissed. "But make sure you don't get spotted."

It was all right for me, I had the mask to hide behind, but I didn't want the others to get caught.

I waited till the others were in position at the side windows, and Frankie gave me a thumbs-up. Then I picked up the mask, and slid it over my head. I got it into position so that I could see through the cut-out eyes, and then I peered through the window at the top of the door. The M&Ms were only a few yards away. In fact, they were so close that I could hear Emma Hughes snoring.

I took a deep breath, and tapped on the glass!

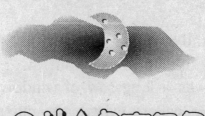

CHAPTER EIGHT

At first, neither of the M&Ms woke up. So I tapped a little bit louder. I was a bit worried I might wake up someone else in the room first, but no-one stirred.

Then Emma Hughes stopped snoring, and started to move about a bit inside her sleeping bag. I tapped again.

Emma opened her eyes, and looked straight at me. I mean, she looked straight at the mummy mask peering in at her through the glass.

Emma's mouth fell open. She looked as if she was trying to scream, but she was so terrified, she couldn't make a sound. I wanted to burst out laughing, but of course I couldn't.

I saw Emma grab Emily's arm. Emily woke up, looked at me and let out a roar that must've woken everyone else in the museum up.

"AAGGGH! IT'S THE MUMMY!!!"

Oh, it was BRILLIANT! They both looked totally scared out of their skins, and Emma Hughes started crying. I wanted to stay and watch them a bit longer, but Mrs Weaver had woken up now, and was putting her dressing gown on. Time to leg it, if we knew what was good for us. I ducked down out of sight, just as Frankie and the others did the same at the other windows.

"Did you see their faces!" Fliss whispered, red-faced from trying not to giggle.

"That's the best trick we've ever done!" said Lyndz.

"And now we've got to get out of here," I said urgently. "Mrs Weaver's awake."

We were just about to make a run for it,

when we heard Mrs Weaver talking inside the room.

"Whatever's the matter, Emma?" we heard her say.

"It was the mummy, Miss!" Emily gasped. Emma was weeping too much to say anything. "It's alive! It was looking through the window at us!"

We all clutched at each other, and bit hard on our lips to stop ourselves laughing.

"Oh really?" Mrs Weaver said in a grim voice. "We'll see!"

And then we heard her walk over to the door. Boy, did we stop laughing straightaway.

"Leg it!" I hissed at the others.

We ran. We skidded off down the corridor at a hundred miles an hour. Luckily we made it round the corner before Mrs Weaver opened the door.

"Who's there?" we heard her say sharply. I prayed that she'd go back in, shut the door and tell the M&Ms that they'd dreamt it. But she didn't. Next thing was, we heard her coming down the corridor after us!

"We've got to get back to our sleeping bags!" Frankie said urgently. "Quick!" She opened the door of one of the galleries. "In here!"

"This isn't the room with the statues that we came through before," I said.

"Never mind, we'll find our way back somehow." Frankie pushed me inside, and the others followed.

The room was in complete darkness.

"Why didn't we bring our torches!" said Rosie. "Where are we?"

"Sssh!" said Lyndz. "I can hear Mrs Weaver going past!"

We all held our breath. Mrs Weaver hurried past the room we were in, and turned the corner.

"I bet she's going to check up on all the other groups," said Frankie. "We've got to get back to the Egyptian Room before she does!"

"It'd help if we could see where we were," I said. I stretched out a hand in the darkness – and it touched something furry. I managed not to scream, but I wasn't far off.

"What is it, Kenny?" asked Rosie, who'd heard me give a little yelp.

"I touched something furry!" I gasped.

"I'm scared!" Fliss moaned. "What is it?"

"If I could see it, I'd tell you!" I snapped. I stretched out my hand again, and felt the furry thing. It was pretty gross feeling something like that in the dark, a bit like that game we play at sleepovers sometimes – you know the one, where someone's blindfolded and you give them really gruesome objects, and they have to guess what they are. I gave Fliss some cold spaghetti once, and told her it was worms. She nearly passed out.

Anyway, I forced myself to keep feeling the furry thing, and then I guessed what it was.

"It's a stuffed animal!" I said, relieved. "I think we're in the animals gallery."

"Ugh! Gross!" said Fliss. "Let's get out of here."

"I think there's a door on the other side," said Frankie. "Hold hands so we can keep together, and I'll see if I can find it."

We inched our way through the darkness,

with Frankie at the front.

"Here's the door," said Frankie, sounding mightily relieved. She pulled it open a little way, and checked the coast was clear. Next second, we were out in the dim light of another corridor.

"Are we lost?" asked Lyndz anxiously.

I tried to think. I knew the museum really well, but right now my brain just wouldn't work.

"I think we go this way," I said, pointing down the corridor. And that was when we heard the noise again. Footsteps, coming towards us. Fliss squealed with fright, and the footsteps started to run.

"Quick, in here!" Frankie opened the door of the nearest room, and bundled us all inside. Fliss's knees were shaking so much, Rosie had to drag her in after the rest of us. This time the room was lit, and we could see it was full of broken old pots, that someone had put back together, like jigsaw puzzles.

"That way!" I hissed frantically, pointing to a door on the other side of the room. We raced over to it on tiptoe. As Frankie pulled it open, we heard the door we'd just come in at start to open!

This time Fliss was too terrified even to make a sound, and the rest of us weren't far behind. We scuttled through the door, and Frankie pulled it shut. There was another gallery opposite us, and I reached for the door handle. I didn't know which room it was, and I didn't care. I just flung the door open.

"Not in there!" gasped Rosie, leaping forward and pulling it shut. Before it closed, I saw why. It was the Science Room, and there were kids from our class in sleeping bags all over the floor.

"What's going on?" we heard someone say sleepily, as Rosie shut the door, and then we heard the sound of torches being switched on.

"Everyone in the museum's going to be awake at this rate!" I said through my teeth. "Frankie, do something!"

Frankie looked as frantic as I was feeling, but she bravely set off down the corridor and

,we all followed. Behind us we heard the sounds of lights being switched on, and people talking.

"Even if we do make it back to our room, Frankie's mum's bound to be awake," Rosie groaned.

"Maybe not," Lyndz said hopefully. "The Egyptian room's right over the other side of the building."

Frankie stopped outside yet another door, labelled "Flower Paintings".

"If we go through here, I think there's a short cut back to the mummies," she said. She didn't sound too sure, but nobody was about to argue. We all bundled into the room, and closed the door behind us.

It was a long room, with old paintings of flowers in big vases along the walls. There were loads of windows, and it was starting to get a bit lighter outside, so at least we could see where we were going now. The only problem was, there were six doors all along the room.

"Which door is it?" asked Fliss through

chattering teeth.

Frankie looked at me, and I looked at Frankie. This was one of the rooms that Mrs Saunders hadn't taken us into on this visit, so we had to try and remember from one of our other trips.

"The one at the end of the room!" we both said together.

"It comes out into another gallery with paintings in it, and that's right opposite the Egyptian room," Frankie added.

The others all sighed with relief. We raced down the long room towards the very last door, and skidded to a halt. But as we got nearer, we could see that there was a sign on the door.

THIS GALLERY IS CLOSED
FOR RE-DECORATION

We all groaned. Rosie reached out, and rattled the handle, but the door was locked.

"What now?" squeaked Fliss. "There must be another way back!"

"We'll have to try one of the other doors," Frankie panted. I'd never seen her look so wound up – she's usually dead cool. Mind you, I wasn't exactly having a laugh myself. I knew just how ballistic Mrs Weaver would go if she caught us!

Frankie yanked open the door nearest to us, and we dived through into another gallery. It was full of those metal suits of armour, all standing up in long rows. Fliss clutched at my hand.

"I hate these," she muttered. "I always think there's really people inside them."

Fliss is a bit of a wimp, but this time I knew what she meant. We were halfway along the corridor, when Fliss, who was still clutching my hand, dug her nails in. Hard.

"Ow!" I tried to pull away from her, but Fliss was hanging onto me like a limpet. "What's biting you?"

"That – that suit of armour," Fliss moaned. "It – it MOVED!"

"Oh, don't be so pathetic!" I snapped, but I couldn't help looking hard at the suit of armour Fliss was pointing at. So did the others. And we all shuffled forward a bit, so that we were huddled close together.

"It did!" Fliss was practically hysterical. "He lifted his hand up! I saw it!"

"Fliss, it's a suit of armour!" said Frankie. "There's no-one inside it. Look."

She reached out, and touched the metal hand. It broke away from the metal arm, and fell to the polished floor with a resounding CRASH that must have woken everybody up for five miles around.

That put the king in the cake. We ran for it. We hurtled out the other side of the gallery, and into the corridor, gasping for breath. Then we saw the sign on the door opposite.

THE EGYPTIAN ROOM

"We've made it!" I gasped. "Let's hope your mum's still asleep, Frankie."

"And that Mrs Weaver's not waiting for us behind the door," said Rosie.

We pushed open the door, hardly daring to breathe. But, unbelievably, everything was exactly the same as we'd left it. And Frankie's mum was still fast asleep in her sleeping bag on the other side of the room.

"I don't believe it!" muttered Fliss. "We did it!"

Then we heard footsteps coming down the corridor. Mrs Weaver was obviously still on the warpath.

"Move!" I hissed.

We all dived into our sleeping-bags. Two seconds later, the door opened!

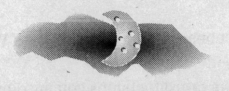

CHAPTER NINE

We all shut our eyes at exactly the same moment that Mrs Weaver looked round the door. She shone her torch into the room, and then we all pretended to wake up.

"Sorry to disturb you, girls," said Mrs Weaver. "But someone's been running around the museum playing tricks."

"Oh, really, Miss?" said Frankie, doing a great imitation of a yawn.

"Is everything all right, Mrs Weaver?" Frankie's mum had got out of her sleeping bag, and come across the room. "Has something happened?"

"Someone's been frightening the girls in my group with a mummy mask," said Mrs Weaver grimly. "I almost caught them, but then I got lost around the galleries."

I glanced at Frankie. So Mrs Weaver had got lost too. That must've been why we made it back before her. Lucky or what?

"Well, I don't think it was any of us," said Frankie's mum, looking round. "We're all here."

"So I see," said Mrs Weaver, 'I think I'll go and check on Ryan Scott's group.' And she closed the door.

"Come on, girls, let's get back to sleep," said Frankie's mum, "or you'll be dead tired in the morning."

We all snuggled down into our sleeping bags. But as soon as Mrs Thomas had gone back over to the other side of the room, we all started laughing and talking. We were just too hyped up to go to sleep right away.

"I can't believe we got back here before Mrs Weaver," whispered Fliss. "We nearly didn't make it!"

"Thank goodness she got lost as well," said Rosie, "or we'd have been nicked!"

"It was worth it though," said Lyndz. "I just wish I had a photo of Emma's face when she saw Kenny in that mask!"

We all started shaking with laughter. The more we tried to stop, the more we laughed. We had to stuff corners of our sleeping-bags in our mouths to stop ourselves from making too much noise.

"We trashed the M&Ms good and proper," I said at last, when we'd finally stopped laughing. "I bet they know it was us, too."

"Do you think so?" said Fliss, looking scared. "What if they tell Mrs Weaver?"

"So what if they do?" said Frankie. "They've got no proof."

"They might have recognised Kenny's mask," said Rosie.

"My mask!" I said suddenly.

"Girls, will you please be quiet and get some sleep?" said Mrs Thomas from across the room.

"What about your mask, Kenny?"

whispered Lyndz.

"I've lost it!" I whispered back. "I put it down somewhere when we were trying to make it back here, and I can't remember where!"

"We've got to get it back!" said Frankie urgently. "If Mrs Weaver finds it—"

"She'll know it was us who played the trick," finished Rosie.

"Where did you leave it, Kenny?" asked Lyndz.

I thought hard.

"I think I put it down on the floor when I was trying to work out what that furry thing was," I said at last. "D'you think I should go and try to get it back now?"

"NO!" said the others all together.

"Girls," said Mrs Thomas, and she was starting to sound pretty annoyed, "will you please go to sleep now."

"We'll look for it first thing tomorrow morning," Frankie whispered, and I nodded.

I wasn't really that worried. After all, somebody else could have borrowed my mask to play a trick on the M&Ms. But I didn't want Mrs Weaver getting suspicious. I wasn't her flavour of the month as it was. I didn't want to get into any more doom.

I yawned and closed my eyes. A picture of Emma and Emily's horrified faces as they looked at the mummy looking in at them came into my mind, and I started giggling into my pillow.

I was still smiling when I fell asleep.

"Kenny?"

Someone was shaking me awake. I didn't want to open my eyes, but whoever it was kept on shaking me, so I had to.

It was Rosie.

"It's ten-to-eight, and we're having breakfast in ten minutes," she said. "I think we should go and look for the mask."

"OK." I rolled out of my sleeping bag, and reached for my jeans. The others were starting to wake up too, except for Frankie, who was snoring. I gave her a kick.

"Wakey, wakey, Francesca."

"Where's my mum?"

"I think she's gone to the loo," said Rosie. "Me and Kenny are going to look for the mask."

We left the others climbing sleepily into their clothes, and headed off down the corridor.

"Let's try the stuffed animals room first," I said. "I'm pretty sure that's where I left it."

It was a lot easier to find our way around the museum in daylight. We went into the animal gallery, and looked round.

"This is gross!" said Rosie, staring at a stuffed peacock. "Why would anyone want to stuff an animal?"

"D'you want to know how they do it?" I said. "First they —"

Rosie gave me a shove. "Not before breakfast, thanks. Why are you such a weirdo, Kenny?"

"I'm just so good at it." I grinned, and took a look round the room. Most of the animals were inside glass cases, but some were just standing around on little platforms.

"I think that fox might have been the furry thing I was touching," I said, pointing across the room.

We went over to it.

"It looks a bit moth-eaten," said Rosie. "Are you sure this was where you left the mask?"

I closed my eyes, and thought hard.

"Yep," I said at last. "I remember I had the mask in one hand, and I touched the fox with the other. I didn't know what it was, so I put the mask down, so I could use both hands."

Rosie looked at me. "Well, where is it then?"

We searched all round where the fox was standing, and then all round the rest of the room, but the mask was nowhere to be seen.

"You must've left it somewhere else," Rosie said at last.

"I didn't." I knew I hadn't. I remembered putting the mask down right next to the stuffed fox. So where had it got to?

"Have you lost something, girls?"

The voice behind us made us jump a mile. We turned round. Frankie's mum was there, carrying a towel and a toothbrush.

"No, Mrs Thomas," I said innocently. "We had a bit of time before breakfast, so we came to look at the animals."

Frankie's mum glanced at her watch.

"Well, it's eight o'clock now, so we'd better go down to the café."

"What are we going to do about the mask?" Rosie whispered in my ear.

I shrugged. "Not a lot. Maybe an early-morning cleaner's chucked it in the bin or something."

We met up with the others in the café. They were already getting stuck into bowls of Coco-Pops and plates of toast.

"Did you find the mask?" was the first question Lyndz asked us.

Rosie and I shook our heads.

"It's gone," I said, "don't ask me where."

"Maybe Mrs Weaver found it," said Fliss, looking terrified.

We all stared hard at Mrs Weaver, who'd just walked in. She looked all right. Meaning, she didn't have steam coming out of her ears.

"Good morning, children," she said, with a smile.

"Looks like we're in the clear," I said to the others. Then we all started to giggle. Behind Mrs Weaver were the M&Ms. They both had black circles under their eyes, and they looked as if they hadn't had any sleep all night.

"Bad night, Emma?" I said, with a huge grin.

"Yeah, we heard about that mummy coming after you," said Frankie. "Funny, we were in the same room with it, and it didn't come after us."

"We didn't even hear it get up and go out," added Rosie, with a totally innocent look on her face. "We were all fast asleep."

The M&Ms looked fit to bust, they were so furious. And that just cracked us up even more.

"We know it was you!" spluttered Emma Hughes. "You're totally pathetic!"

"And we're going to tell Mrs Weaver!" growled Emily Berryman.

"Go on then," I challenged them coolly. "You've got no proof."

The M&Ms opened and shut their mouths a few times like a couple of angry goldfish, but they knew I was right. Mrs Weaver wouldn't give them the time of day, unless they could prove for certain that it was us who'd played that trick on them.

"Hey, Emma!" Ryan Scott and his mate Danny McCloud walked into the café with their hands held out in front of them like a couple of zombies. "We've risen from the dead, and we're coming to get you!"

We all fell about. The Queen and the Goblin were going to be the joke of the whole school for the next few weeks, and didn't they deserve it. They both turned bright red, and stalked off.

"Result!" I said, holding up my hand to Frankie for a high five. Then I did the same to all the others. What a radical sleepover that had been. I'd never thought my idea would work out so brilliantly.

"More toast, anyone?" said a voice from behind us. It was Frankie's mum. That shut us all up.

"You've obviously had a good time, then," Mrs Thomas remarked after she'd handed round the toast.

"Yes, we have," we all chorused politely. She just didn't know how good.

Mrs Thomas looked pleased.

"Good. Well, when you've finished eating, go and pack your stuff away, and collect your masks. The coach is coming at nine to pick us up."

"I wish I knew where my mask had gone," I moaned to Frankie as we packed our sleeping bags away after breakfast. "I wanted to keep it as a souvenir of the night we crushed the M&Ms."

"What were you going to do, frame it and stick it on your bedroom wall?" Rosie asked.

"Something like that." I grinned evilly. "I was thinking about trying the same trick on Molly Monster-Features."

Just then Fliss and Lyndz, who'd gone to collect Fliss's mask, came in, carrying a black bin-liner. Frankie's mum was behind them.

"The coach is here, girls," she said. "Kenny,

have you collected your mask?"

That threw me. I stared at Frankie's mum, and for a second, I couldn't think of anything to say.

It was Fliss who saved the day.

"I've got the masks here, Mrs Thomas," she said, waving the black bin liner.

"Right, let's go then." Frankie's mum picked up her bags, and went out, while the rest of us sagged with relief.

"Nice one, Flissy," I said gratefully. "Thanks."

Fliss turned pink. "I'm not as stupid as I look," she said.

"No, of course not," I agreed. "Nobody could be that stupid."

We all cracked up at that, even Fliss. We picked up our bags, and I took one last look around the room.

"I wish I hadn't lost that mask," I muttered. "I don't suppose I'll ever see it again now."

Guess what? I was wrong!

CHAPTER TEN – GOODBYE

So now I've told you almost everything that happened at the Great Museum Sleepover. Almost. But not quite.

We decided that we'd all go round to Frankie's on Saturday afternoon, so that we could talk over what had happened. Oh, and to have a good laugh at the M&Ms, of course.

It was a sunny day, so Frankie's dad had put their sun lounger out on the patio. It was one of those swinging ones, and we all piled onto it, even though it was a bit small for the five of us. It's really old as well, so it creaked every time we swung it backwards and forwards.

"I can't wait till Monday," said Fliss.

"Everyone in the whole school's going to know what happened to the M&Ms."

"And if they don't, we'll soon tell them," I said, swinging the sun lounger to and fro a little bit faster. Rosie, who was squashed in the middle and had hardly any seat at all, flew off as the seat swung back, and landed on the patio on her bottom.

"Ow!" she complained, while the rest of us howled with laughter. "Can't somebody else sit in the middle?"

We all squashed up, so that Rosie could get in on the end. Now Fliss was in the middle. I raised my eyebrows at Frankie. "How long to knock Fliss off the seat, and onto the patio?"

"Six seconds," said Frankie.

"What?" asked Fliss.

"Nothing," I said. "I don't reckon we'll get any bother from the M&Ms now for a while, do you?"

"They'll want to get their own back sometime," Lyndz said. "I've never seen Emma Hughes that mad."

"We'll be ready for them," I said, swinging the seat back as hard as I could. Fliss gave a squeal, and slid off onto the patio with a thump.

"Five seconds," said Frankie, looking at her watch. "Good one."

"Very funny," sniffed Fliss, climbing to her feet.

"What are we going to do this afternoon then?" asked Lyndz.

"Let's just sit around and talk," suggested Frankie. "I'll make us some Coca-Cola floats."

"Cool!" I said. "And I'll show you my impression of Emma Hughes' face when she saw the mummy. I've been practising it since yesterday."

I pulled open my mouth and popped out my eyes as far as they would go. The others howled.

"And this is Emily Berryman." I stopped, and put on a really deep, gruff voice. "HELP! THE MUMMY! IT'S ALIVE!!!"

I didn't get to finish my impression of Emily, because Frankie's mum came into the garden out of their garage. She was wearing old clothes and rubber gloves, and she had a black bin-liner in her hand.

"Frankie, if you girls want anything to eat, you'll have to get it yourself," Mrs Thomas said. "I'm going to make a start on cleaning out the garage."

She didn't look too happy about it, and I wasn't surprised. Frankie's family are like squirrels. They keep everything. The garage has so many boxes and bags in it that they have to park their car on the drive.

"Oh, by the way," said Mrs Thomas, "I thought you might like this."

She opened the bin-liner, and pulled out a cardboard mask. A mummy mask. My mask.

"I think it's yours, isn't it, Kenny?"

I was too gobsmacked to say anything, and so were the others. I just nodded.

"I found it in the stuffed animals gallery this morning," Frankie's mum went on. "Funny. I can't think how it got there!"

This time it was us who looked like goldfish. We opened our mouths, couldn't think of anything to say, and shut them again. Frankie's mum put the mask back in the bin-liner, and gave it to me. I knew then that she knew. Mrs Thomas knew that it was *us* who'd played that trick the night before.

The question was, what was she going to do about it?

"Well, I think I'd better get on with clearing the garage," said Frankie's mum. "Of course, I'd get on a lot quicker if you girls gave me a hand!"

"We'd love to," we all said together.

"It's a bit of a dirty job, and it's going to take a while," Mrs Thomas pointed out. "Sure you don't mind?"

"Oh, we don't mind," I said. "Not one bit."

Frankie's mum went back into the garage, and we all looked at each other.

"She knows!" babbled Fliss nervously.

"And she's let us off," Rosie added.

"Not quite," said Frankie. "You haven't seen our garage."

"Your mum knew the M&Ms played that trick on Kenny," said Lyndz. "That must be why she didn't give us away."

"Your mum's really cool, Frankie," I said.

"Yeah, but we'd better not push it," Frankie warned us, sliding off the sun lounger. "Come on, let's get started."

So that was what I mean when I said we'd sort of got away with it. Although after an afternoon clearing out Frankie's garage, I think I'd rather have been grounded for a week. It was cool of Mrs Thomas not to give us away though. Mrs Weaver would have chewed us to bits if she'd found out.

That's it. End of story. I didn't do so badly, did I? I was just as good as Frankie.

Look, there are the others over there by the playground gate. Come over, and say hello. Oh, and here come the M&Ms, with their faces down to their knees. I'm really going to enjoy this. I've been looking through all my joke books, and finding loads of jokes about mummies, so that I can annoy the Gruesome Twosome all day.

I'll catch up with you again really soon.

By-e-e-e-e!

The Sleepover Club at Frankie's

Join the Sleepover Club: Frankie, Kenny, Felicity, Rosie and Lyndsey, five girls who just want to have fun – but who always end up in mischief.

Brown Owl's in a bad mood and the Sleepover Club are determined to cheer her up. Maybe she'd be happier if she had a new boyfriend. And where better than a sleepover at Frankie's to plan Operation Blind Date?

Pack up your sleepover kit and drop in on the fun!

0 00 675233 0
£2. 99

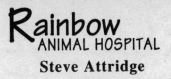

Rainbow
ANIMAL HOSPITAL
Steve Attridge

Sick pets and injured animals –
every day brings a new emergency for Eddie
and the staff at the Rainbow Animal Hospital.

Bartholomew the Champion

When a huge Bernese Mountain Dog with a broken
leg fails to get better, only Eddie realises what's
wrong. He and his brilliant little sister Kate
come up with a daring plan to save the dog's life.
It could get them into serious trouble but that's
a risk they have to take – for Bartholomew's sake.

If you care about animals and
love adventure stories,

Rainbow
ANIMAL HOSPITAL

is for you.

Collins

Order Form

To order direct from the publishers, just make a list of the titles you want and fill in the form below:

Name

....

Address

....

....

....

Send to: Dept 6, HarperCollins Publishers Ltd, Westerhill Road, Bishopbriggs, Glasgow G64 2QT.

Please enclose a cheque or postal order to the value of the cover price, plus:

UK & BFPO: Add £1.00 for the first book, and 25p per copy for each additional book ordered.

Overseas and Eire: Add £2.95 service charge. Books will be sent by surface mail but quotes for airmail despatch will be given on request.

A 24-hour telephone ordering service is available to holders of Visa, MasterCard, Amex or Switch cards on 0141- 772 2281.

Collins
An *Imprint* of HarperCollins*Publishers*